STORYLAND

Classic Tales For Children

Retold by Howard Hall

Illustrated by Rene Cloke

AWARD PUBLICATIONS

The Three Little Pigs

There were three little pigs called Grunter,
Porker and Squeaky who lived on a farm. All
the animals on the farm were very happy
together until one day the farmer sold the
farm.

"What shall we do?" cried Porker. "We'll just
have to leave, and build homes for ourselves!"
replied Squeaky. So the three little pigs went
off to pack their bags. As they said 'Goodbye'
to their friends the sheepdog warned: "Watch
out for the wicked Grey Wolf!"

Carrying their bags, the three little pigs
walked down the farm track into the
countryside.

Now Porker had always liked the smell of
fresh straw.
He liked the smell so much he decided to
build a house out of straw. So he left
his friends and went to see a corn
farmer who sold him some bundles of straw.
Porker soon set to work. The straw was
light and easy to carry.
By noon the house was finished.
But he'd been so busy, he didn't see
Grey Wolf come creeping along.

With one big *PUFF*
the wolf blew
Porker's house down.

Meanwhile, Grunter and Squeaky were
walking by the wood. They hadn't
walked very far when they met a boy
selling sticks.
"That's given me an idea," said Grunter.
"I think I'll build my house out of sticks".
"Good luck! I'll come and visit you soon!"
cried Squeaky.

With the help of two fieldmice, Grunter
built his house out of sticks.
He worked so hard that his house was
almost finished by dinner time.
He had just painted the front door
when Grey Wolf crept out of the woods.
"Three PUFFS and I'll eat you for dinner!"
growled Grey Wolf.

Grunter locked the door in fright.
But Grey Wolf blew. And the third
time he blew, poor Grunter's house
fell down.
Grunter ran away as fast as his legs
could carry him.

Only Squeaky remembered the sheepdog's
warning about Grey Wolf. So he built
his house with bricks and cement.
Squeaky carefully cemented the bricks
together so that the walls of his house
were thick and strong.
Squeaky worked very hard and two little
songbirds sang beautiful melodies as he
built his house of brick.
It was growing dark by the time Squeaky
had finished. He was really glad to
lock the front door and go upstairs to bed.
He had just put out the light when there
was a knock on the door.
Squeaky opened the window and looked out...

8

Squeaky shivered with fright when he saw
Grey Wolf standing on the garden path.
"What do you want?" asked Squeaky.
"May I come in?" asked the wolf, licking
his lips.
"No you can't come in," answered Squeaky.
"But I'm very hungry," said the wolf.
"I have no food for wolves," answered
Squeaky. "Only turnips."
"Turnips?" cried the crafty wolf...

"If its turnips you like," said the wolf:
"I know a turnip field by the rabbit warren.
The turnips there are delicious. Why not
meet me there at seven o'clock tomorrow
morning?"
"Alright Mr Wolf," yawned Squeaky. "I'll
meet you there at seven."
Licking his lips, the wolf crept away.
"At seven I'll have a nice tasty pig for
breakfast!" he chuckled.
Of course Squeaky didn't want to see the
nasty wolf again. So he stayed in bed
until *ten*.

When Squeaky arrived at the turnip field
the wolf had gone, and Squeaky was able
to eat two nice turnips in peace.
Later he made friends with some rabbits
who told him where he could find some
delicious apples. "You'll find them in
the old orchard where the red squirrels
live," they said.
"In the afternoon I'll go to the orchard,"
decided Squeaky. "I only hope I don't
meet the wolf there."

Squeaky was sitting
in the orchard
eating an apple
when the wolf came.
But before the wolf could
even lick his lips,
Squeaky threw him
an apple.

"Try an apple Mr Wolf!" he squeaked.
"They're really delicious!"

As the wolf turned to chase
the apple, Squeaky slid down the
tree and ran all the way home.

Squeaky was very pleased with his new home. He soon made friends with all the squirrels and rabbits and the songbirds in the neighbourhood. But he really missed his old pals Grunter and Porker pig.

"I hope Grunter and Porker will visit me soon", he said. "We'll have so much to talk about."

One day when the fair came to a nearby hill, Squeaky decided to go.

"I might meet Porker and Grunter there," he said, "unless that nasty Grey Wolf has gobbled them up."

Squeaky had a lovely time at the fair. As he rode on the roundabout he forgot all about the nasty wolf. He even won a balloon and a wooden barrel to keep his turnips in.

"Its just what I needed!" he squeaked. "What a wonderful day it has been!"

Squeaky was singing a song and carrying his barrel home, when he suddenly had a horrible fright.

Just ahead of him he saw Grey Wolf! The wolf was climbing up the hill towards the fair, and in a second or two he would see Squeaky. Squeaky was so scared he let go of his balloon!

16

For a moment poor Squeaky just stood
there.
What could he do?
It was almost too late to hide.
Then Squeaky had a clever idea.
He climbed into the barrel and put
on the lid.
Slowly the turnip barrel began to roll
towards the wolf...

Once the turnip barrel reached the hill
it rolled faster and faster.
And what is more, it rolled *straight*
towards Grey Wolf.
"Its chasing me!" growled the wolf.
"I'd better run!"
So the wolf ran off down the hill.
The barrel travelled so fast at one point
that it flew through the air, frightening
the wolf even more.

At the bottom of the hill, the wooden
barrel stopped. Squeaky lifted off
the lid and crawled out. Grey
Wolf was nowhere to be seen.
"I've just frightened the wolf!" laughed
Squeaky.
"You frightened me too Squeaky!" cried
a rabbit. "And once Grey Wolf hears
it was you inside the barrel, he'll be
very angry!"
But for once Squeaky didn't care.

When Squeaky arrived home he could have
danced with joy!
Porker and Grunter had arrived! They
were standing in the garden waiting
for him.
"Grey Wolf blew our houses down,"
they explained. "He would have eaten
us too if he'd caught us. And we're
so glad you're safe and well."
"You must both stay here," said Squeaky.
"The wolf can't blow this house down
because it's made of brick and cement."
"But he's sure to come back when he
knows there are *three* pigs here,"
said Porker.
"Then we must lock the door and keep the
windows tightly shut," said Squeaky. "And
cheer up! I've gathered some turnips. If
you light the fire Porker, we can have a
nice turnip soup. Then we can talk about
our adventures since we left the farm."

The big soup pot was bubbling on the
fire and the three little pigs were
looking forward to their meal. They had
forgotten all about the wolf when there
was a loud knock on the door.
"Its the wolf!" yelped Porker.
"He's come to eat us!"
grunted Grunter.
"What do you want
Mr Wolf?" asked Squeaky.

"I want to come in,"
growled the wolf.
"You *must* let me in.
I'm very hungry!"

"You can't come in," said Squeaky.
"If you don't open the door," warned
the wolf, "I'll climb onto the roof
and come down the chimney pot!"
The next moment the three little pigs
heard the wolf climbing onto the roof.
Then they heard him growl down the
chimney pot.
"The chimney pot!" squealed Porker.
"He's coming down the chimney pot.
And we'll all be eaten alive!"

The pigs listened as the wolf began
to climb down the chimney.
Porker and Grunter were frozen with terror.
In a second or two the wolf would be in the
room and they'd all be eaten alive!

But at the very *last* moment,
Squeaky walked to the fireplace.
As the wolf appeared, Squeaky lifted the
lid off the soup pot.
The nasty Grey Wolf dropped straight
into the boiling soup.
"That's the end of the wolf!"
Squeaked Squeaky.

It was the end of the wolf –
but not the end of the three little
pigs.
Grunter and Porker built their houses
next to Squeaky's.
And every Friday night they cook
themselves a big pot of turnip soup!

The Three Bears

As Goldilocks walked through the
woods she smelt a delicious smell.
Someone was cooking porridge, and
Goldilocks loved porridge!
Goldilocks didn't know that the three bears
lived in the wood. And it was their
porridge she could smell.
The three bears lived in a great
big hollow tree. It was so big
inside the tree that the three
bears had made their home there.
Mother Bear had just served up the
porridge when Father Bear said: "Let's
go for a short walk. When we get back
the porridge will be ready to eat!"
"That's a very good idea," agreed
Mother Bear. "And I can collect some
berries on the way."
So off they plodded. Big Daddy Bear,
followed by medium-sized Mummy Bear,
followed by tiny little Baby Bear.

26

A few moments later, Goldilocks
came to the great big tree where
the three bears lived.
Goldilocks had never seen a front
door in a tree before.
She was so curious that she opened
the tree door and stepped inside
the house of the three bears...

On the kitchen table
were three bowls
of porridge:
There was a big bowl.
A medium-sized bowl.
And a tiny wee bowl.

Seeing the bowls of steaming porridge made
Goldilocks feel very hungry.
She was so hungry that she tried a
spoonful of the porridge in the big bowl.
But it was far too salty.
Next, Goldilocks tried the medium-sized
bowl. This porridge was too sweet.
Last of all, Goldilocks tried the tiny bowl.

Goldilocks liked the taste of the
porridge in the tiny bowl.
In fact it was so delicious that Goldilocks
ate it all!
Then she thought: "I wonder whose
house this is? I wonder whose porridge
I have been eating?"

Goldilocks walked into another room
in the three bears' house and saw a
great big chair.
"I'm so tired," sighed Goldilocks.
"I think I'll sit down in this chair."
But the big chair was Daddy Bear's
chair and much too big for Goldilocks.
"I wonder if I can find a smaller chair,"
sighed Goldilocks.

In another room inside the hollow tree,
Goldilocks found a medium-sized chair.
By the chair was a window with a
lovely view of the woods.
"It will be nice to sit here," said
Goldilocks.
But when she sat on the medium-sized
chair she found that it was a very hard.
"Perhaps there is a softer chair
somewhere?" she sighed.

In little Baby Bear's room,
Goldilocks found a tiny chair.
It was soft too. What's more,
Goldilocks found it very pleasant
to sit on.
But Goldilocks was too heavy for
the tiny chair...
The chair broke! And Goldilocks fell
on the floor!
She was lucky not to hurt herself!

Goldilocks picked herself
up and started up
the stairs.

She was so sorry
to have broken the chair.
But she was still very tired.
"I wonder what is up these stairs?"
she thought to herself. "Perhaps I
might find a bed there to lie on."

It really was the strangest house
Goldilocks had ever been in!
Who would believe her if she said she
had been in a lovely house *inside* a
great big tree?
Some of the branches of the tree
actually grew inside the house. On the
wall by the stair were ornaments,
some of brass and some of china.
The stairs were nice and clean and
everything smelt as fresh as a forest
on a spring day.

As Goldilocks climbed the stairs she
was beginning to wish she lived in
such a pleasant house.
She was yawning as she came to a
green door right at the top.
Having walked so far and eaten such nice
porridge, she was feeling very sleepy
indeed. All she wanted to do now
was to lie down and rest...

Goldilocks
opened
the door.

Inside the room were three lovely beds.
Each of the beds looked so inviting.

36

There was a big bed.
A medium-sized bed.
And a tiny little bed.
Each of the beds was covered in a
beautiful eiderdown that had been
made by Mother Bear.
The big bed belonged to Father Bear.
The medium-sized bed belonged to
Mother Bear.

Goldilocks tried the big bed first.
But it was too hard!
So Goldilocks tried the medium-sized bed.
But *it* was too soft.
Finally, Goldilocks lay down on the little
bed.
It was just right!
It was just like her bed at home!

There was a cuddly teddy bear at the top
of the bed.
As Goldilocks closed her eyes she
wondered whose teddy bear it was.
And whose bed she was lying in...?
Only a few moments passed before
Goldilocks fell into a deep sleep
in Baby Bear's bed.

Meanwhile, the three bears were on their way home. They had had a very pleasant walk in the woods and now they were all looking forward to their breakfast.

"Our porridge should be ready to eat by now," said Father Bear in his big deep voice. Father Bear had found a stout walking stick in the wood and he was very pleased with it. "This is just what I've been looking for!" he boomed.

"Yes," said Mother Bear in a softer voice. "And I've found these lovely coloured berries to hang over the fireplace. Won't they look nice?"

"Yes they will," squeaked Baby Bear in his tiny voice. "And I've found a wooden hoop which I will put in my playroom." Suddenly Father Bear stopped. The door of their tree house was standing open...

"I'm sure I closed the door when we left," he said.

"I do believe that someone has been inside our house!" growled Father Bear as he entered the porch.

"I wonder who it can be?" said Mother Bear anxiously.

"I do hope they haven't eaten my porridge, because I'm *very* hungry!" said Baby Bear.

But someone had eaten Baby Bear's porridge,
And that wasn't all!

"Someone has been
sitting in my chair!"
boomed Father Bear.

"And in my chair too!" said Mother Bear.
"Oh!" cried Baby Bear. "Someone has been
sitting in my chair. And they've broken it!"
"Who can it be?" gasped Mother Bear.
"Who has eaten Baby Bear's porridge and
broken Baby Bear's chair?"
The three bears were gathered around Baby
Bear's chair when suddenly, Father Bear
heard a noise upstairs...

"Someone is in the house!" boomed
Father Bear. "Someone is in our bedroom!"
"I do hope they're not sleeping in
my bed!" cried Mother Bear.
"And I hope they haven't hurt my teddy
bear!" squeaked Baby Bear.

Father Bear opened the bedroom door
and the three bears saw Goldilocks sitting
sleepily on Baby Bear's bed.
She had been woken up by Father Bears deep
voice. "Who are you?" asked Mother Bear.
"And what are you doing sleeping in Baby
Bear's bed?"
Goldilocks was *so* frightened!
She had never seen a *real* bear before!
So she ran quickly past the three bears
and hurried down the stairs...

As Goldilocks ran down the stairs and out of the door, the three bears just stood and stared. They couldn't believe their eyes!

No one, apart from Uncle Bear, had ever been in their house before!

"She must have eaten my porridge!" said Baby Bear.
"And broken your chair!" boomed Father Bear.

Goldilocks ran,
and ran, and ran...
She ran as fast as
her legs could carry her.

Goldilocks didn't stop running until she was nearly home.

It would be the last time Goldilocks would walk into someone else's house without being asked.

And of course, Goldilocks told no one where she had been, for no one would believe a tale about three bears who lived in a tree!

As for the three Bears..

They made some more porridge.
And mended Baby Bear's chair.
And lived happily ever after in their secret home in the great big tree.

The Adventures of Tom Thumb

"Last night I dreamed we had a child,"
sighed the farmer's wife. "But he was
no bigger than a pencil!"
"I'd not mind if he were no bigger than

my thumb!" cried the farmer. "If only
we had a child!"
In the twinkling of an eye, a tiny boy
appeared in the farmer's hand. The
boy was no bigger than the farmer's thumb!
And he'd been sent to them from heaven!

The happy farmer's wife made the boy a
bed out of a pea pod, and clothes out
of coloured ribbons.

The farmer made the child coloured balls
out of dried peas, and a boat out of a
walnut shell.
The farmer and his wife were so happpy with
their gift from heaven. And they called
their tiny child Tom Thumb.

One bright day the farmer had to take his
horse and cart to market. But he wasn't
feeling too well. His wife told him to
rest but the farmer said: "I must take
the horse and cart to market today. It
is *very* important."
Suddenly Tom Thumb piped up: "Sit me in
the horse's ear," he said. "And I will
drive the horse to market. When I
want the horse to stop I'll shout, 'Whoa!'
And when I want the horse to trot, I'll
shout 'Giddy-up!'"

So the farmer sat Tom in the horse's ear...
The people who saw the cart passing by
couldn't believe their eyes!
They thought the horse and cart were
being driven by magic!
Tom Thumb drove the cart all the way to
market – and back home again.
The farmer's wife was so pleased with her
tiny child that she baked him a tiny cake.

One day two men saw
Tom Thumb sitting on
a toadstool near
the farmer who was
chopping wood.

"I'll give you a gold
coin for the tiny imp,"
offered one man.

The farmer was about to refuse,but Tom
said: "Please let me go. It will be an
adventure for me. Later I'll escape and
come back home to you."
So the man gave the farmer a gold coin,
picked up Tom and set him on his hat brim.
Tom had a fine view from the hat brim as
the men walked along. But when he heard
that the men were going to sell him at
the Fair, Tom grew frightened. So when
the tall man took off his hat, Tom jumped
off the hat brim, and ran away.

Tom ran as fast as he could through the
tall grass.
How he wished he could stride along like
a tall man!
As the sun grew hot he found his way into
a mousehole which seemed as big as a cave
to Tom.
Here he made friends with a mouse who gave
him some wild corn to eat. Later Tom
rested before continuing his journey home.

Tom's bedroom during the night
was an empty snail's shell
which sheltered him from
the wind. He used an old leaf
as a mattress, and found
it very comfortable.

The next day, after a long walk, Tom Thumb
arrived back home. The farmer and his wife
were so pleased to see Tom!
But later in the day Tom had an accident!
He was climbing upon the table when he slid
down a spoon into
the pudding basin. The
farmer's wife didn't
see Tom and put
the pudding in the bag.

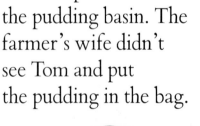

Next the farmer's wife put the pudding bag
into the cooking pot which was simmering
on the fire. Tom began to jump up
and down inside the pudding bag!
It was so *hot!* The farmer's wife, not
knowing that Tom was inside, thought that
there was something wrong with the pudding!
So she gave it to a passing tramp.
Luckily, Tom was able to escape when the
tramp opened the bag. And by evening he was
back again with the farmer and his wife.

One fine day, the farmer's wife took Tom with
her when she went to milk the cows.

The sky was blue and the wind was scented
with summer flowers. It was a beautiful day...
The farmer's wife was worried that a cow
might accidentally tread on Tom, so she
tied Tom to a thistle with a piece of ribbon.
Tom enjoyed sitting there in the soft breeze.
The thistle gently rocked in the wind like
a swing. And Tom grew sleepy.
The farmer's wife seemed to be taking
such a long time.
Eventually Tom fell asleep and he dreamed
he was going to have a great adventure...
Later he woke, and began to sing a song.
Tom's voice sounded like a silver flute.
One of the cows pricked up it's ears at such
a lovely sound.
As the thistle swayed to and fro and Tom
sang, a beautiful blue butterfly came along...
It too had heard Tom sing and liked the sound.
So the blue butterfly hovered near Tom as he
sang and listened to the song.

Tom smiled at
the butterfly.
And the butterfly
smiled back at Tom.

Then a friendly cow came along to where
Tom was sitting on the thistle.
"Please can you teach me to sing?" said the cow.
"I'll try," said Tom. "But first you'll
need to think of a tune you'd like to sing".
"Very well," said the cow. "I think I'd
like to sing 'Hey Diddle Diddle'..."
But when the cow opened its mouth to sing
it blew Tom Thumb straight off the thistle
and into the grass!

As Tom Thumb scampered through the grass
looking for the farmer's wife, a hawk
saw him. Now Tom looked as small as a
mouse to the hawk. So the hawk swooped
down and plucked Tom out of the grass.
Before Tom knew what was happening he felt
himself flying through the air at great speed.

The hawk flew on and on, until Tom could
see the sea below.
"Help!" cried Tom. "Help! Please put me
down!" The hawk was amazed to hear Tom speak.
He was so amazed that he dropped Tom in
surprise. Poor Tom fell with a splash
straight into the sea! The water was very
deep and very cold.

"Help!" cried Tom. "I can't swim."
Tom swallowed lots of salty water and he
felt himself sinking. "I'm drowning," he
thought to himself. "I'll never see the
farmer's wife or the farmer again.
I do wish I hadn't tried to teach that
cow to sing! And I wish I could be saved
just this once!" As Tom was thinking that,
he was swallowed by a great big fish! Inside
it was dark and cold. But at least it was dry...

Tom didn't feel very well at all!
He had swallowed so much water.
And now it was cold and dark.
Tom was just about to take his boots off
when the fish he was in was caught
by a fisherman on the shore.
Suddenly the fish was flying through the
air towards the shore...

Inside the fish, Tom closed his eyes.
Everything was so quiet and still. And it was
very dark. Tom tried shouting for help. But
no one came to rescue him.
Then Tom began to feel frightened.
He imagined he was in a dungeon at
the bottom of the sea.
He began to shiver. It was certainly
cold enough to be a dungeon.
After a time, poor Tom began to feel
very weary. So he lay down inside the
fish, and after a long time he fell asleep.
Meanwhile, the big fish had been taken
to a fishmongers. But when the fishmonger
saw the big fish he said: "This is a fish
fit for a king to eat!" And he had the
big fish sent at once to the palace.
That evening the King's cook began to
prepare the Royal meal. The King's cook
had just cut open the fish when Tom Thumb
woke up. When Tom climbed out

of the fish the cook couldn't believe his eyes!
"My Goodness! Who are you?!" cried the cook.
"I've never seen anyone so small in my
life!" "My name is Tom Thumb," said Tom.
"And who, may I ask, are you?"
"I'm the King's cook," said the man. "And
you've just climbed out of the King's fish!
I *must* show you to the King and Queen!"

The cook put Tom on a plate and took him before
the King and Queen. "Excuse me your Majesty,"
said the cook. "But look what I've found
inside the Royal fish."
"Well bless my soul!" cried the king. "It's
a tiny wee man!"
The Queen clapped her hands with delight as Tom
bowed to the Royal Family. And the King said:
"Well bless my soul!" over and over again!

After Tom had bowed to the Royal Family,
he said: "Good King and Queen, my name
is Tom Thumb. And I'm the son of a poor
farmer who lives many miles from here.
I've had lots of adventures," Tom went
on. "I've dined with a mouse and slept
in a snail's shell at midnight. And I've
also sat in the ear of a horse. But now
I'd just like to go home please."

"And so you shall," promised the King. "But
first we shall hold a party in your honour.
Then we will invite the farmer and his wife to
the palace to collect you." "Thank you very
much your Majesty!" said Tom.
Later that day, Tom Thumb entertained the
Royal children. He did handstands and danced.
Afterwards he sang a song in his sweet voice
all about his adventures. As a special farewell
present, the King gave Tom a dolls house to live
in. The following day Tom returned home with
the happy farmer and his wife.

Puss In Boots

There was once a miller who had three sons:
Peter, John and Robin.
When the miller died he left his money
to Peter. His mill he left to John.
To his youngest son Robin, he left only
a cat.
This cat's name was Puss.
And Puss was a very special cat.

"You're a nice old cat," said Robin to
Puss. "But how am I going to feed us
both? I have no money and no job."
"I may be able to help," purred Puss.
"But I'll need a pair of boots and a hat,
and perhaps a coat if you have one."
"One last thing," added Puss. "Get me
an old sack too. Then just leave
everything to me."

Robin found a hat for
Puss, and a sack.

And with his last few coins he bought
Puss some yellow boots...

The very next day Puss went for a walk
with the sack over his shoulder.
As he walked he tried to think of a plan.
On his way he saw a piece
of rope lying near
a rabbit warren.
"That's given me an idea," said Puss.
"All I need now is a
stick and a sprig
of parsley."

Within an hour Puss
had found a stick
and a sprig of parsley...

Puss in Boots stopped by a tree.
Inside the sack he put the sprig of
parsley. Puss kept the bag open with the
stick. And to the stick he tied the rope.
Then he hid behind the tree.
A woodpecker perched in the tree couldn't
understand what Puss was doing. So he
waited to see what would happen next...

Soon three rabbits came bobbing along.
The first rabbit stopped near the sack...
"I can smell parsley," he said.
"No use just smelling it," said the
second rabbit. "Let's eat it!"

The three rabbits
crept inside the bag
and nibbled the parsley.

Puss waited until they
were all inside, then
he pulled the rope
and caught all three
rabbits in the sack.

After combing the feather in his hat,
Puss polished his yellow boots.
Then he lifted the sack full of rabbits
over his shoulder.
"Now my next plan is to go to see the
King," he purred to himself. "I've
heard his Majesty is very fond of rabbits."

When Puss had walked to the palace, he
knocked at the gate.
And because the guards hadn't seen a cat
in boots before, they let him in.
Next Puss saw one of the King's ministers
who didn't know what to make of a Puss
in boots.
Finally, Puss was taken in to see the King.

80

Puss took off his hat and bowed very low
before speaking...
"Your Majesty," purred Puss. "I have been
sent on a very special mission by my master.
He sends his respectful greetings, and asks
me to bring you a small gift."

Puss opened the bag with the rabbits inside.
The King smiled when he saw the rabbits.
"And who is your master?" asked the King.
"The Marquis of Carabas," replied Puss.
"Well," said the King. "Thank your master for
his gift. The rabbits will be most welcome."

That night Puss in Boots slept in a barn.
He didn't bother going home to see Robin
because he wanted to stay near the palace.
The next day Puss in Boots made another
trap, using the same stick, rope and sack.
This trap he set in the woods, and inside
the sack Puss sprinkled some grains of
golden corn. He took one end of the rope
and hid behind a tree.
Two plump woodpigeons saw the corn, and
when they entered the sack to feed, Puss
tugged on the rope and caught the
woodpigeons in the sack.
Next Puss sent the woodpigeons to the King,
with a note which read: "To the King. From
the Marquis of Carabas."
Later Puss heard that the King was to make
a journey in his Royal carriage. And with
the King would be the Princess, the beautiful
Rose-Marie.
Puss made his plans...

Without saying anything to Robin,
Puss took him swimming near to
where the royal coach was to cross
the river. So he was in the
water when the carriage crossed
over the nearby bridge

Puss suddenly cried:
"Oh Help! Please help!
Someone has stolen my
masters clothes!" The
King leaned out of the
window and ordered the
driver to stop at once.
"Help!" cried Puss again.
"Someone has stolen my master's clothes!"

When the King saw Puss standing there he
remembered the gift of the rabbits and the
woodpigeons.

"That must be the Marquis of Carabas in the river," said the King. "I must help at once, for he has been a good friend to me."

"The Marquis of Carabas must come with me at once!" cried the King.
"I will give him a fresh change of clothing."
"Your Majesty is so kind," purred Puss, bowing low.
When Robin was dressed in Royal clothes, he looked just like a young Prince. And when he bowed to Princess Rose-Marie she fell in love with him.
"I'm proud to know the Marquis of Carabas," she smiled.

Robin really didn't know what to say.
He only hoped Puss knew what he was doing.
But Puss was a clever cat.
He was already planning his next move.
In fact, even as Robin was changing into
dry clothes, Puss was running on ahead
of the carriage.
He ran until he came
upon some workers
in the fields.
"If anyone passes by in
a carriage," cried Puss,
"please tell them that
these fields belong to the
Marquis of Carabas. You'll
be rewarded if you say that!"

Puss ran on until he
came upon a farmer.
"If the Royal carriage
passes by," said Puss, "tell the King and Princess
that these fields belong to the Marquis of Carabas."
"But they belong to the Ogre!" gasped the
farmer. "If he hears of this he'll be very angry!"
"Tonight these fields really *will* belong to the
Marquis of Carabas!" promised Puss. "So please
do what I ask." "Very well," agreed the farmer,
"but I hope you know what you are doing."

Puss ran on through a wood until he reached
the castle where the wicked Ogre lived.
Everyone lived in fear of the Ogre.
It was said that he had the power to
change himself into any creature he wanted...
Puss was running up the steps of the castle
when the gigantic figure of the Ogre loomed
ahead. The Ogre carried a great big club
and glared at Puss as if he
would eat him for supper.
"Hello Mr Ogre!" said Puss.
"Who are you?" growled
the Ogre. "And what is
more to the point – what
do you want?"

"Oh, I'm just an ordinary cat," said Puss.
"But I heard that you were a very clever man."
"I *am* a very clever man!" boomed the Ogre.
"I'm the cleverest man in the whole world!
I'm also the nastiest, and the biggest, and
last, but not least: I'm also a magician!"
"A magician!" gasped Puss. "I've always
wanted to meet a magician! Can you make
things disappear, and can you pull rabbits
out of a hat?"
"Any magician can do that!" growled the Ogre.
"But *I* can change myself into a rabbit, or
even a tiger! In fact, I can do anything
I want to do!"
"I'll bet you can't change youself into
a mouse!" sneered Puss. "Of course I
can change myself into a mouse. What
colour mouse would you like?"
"Oh, any colour will do," said Puss.
"Right! Just you watch!" laughed the Ogre.
"Just you *watch !*"

There was a puff of smoke, and the Ogre
vanished. Puss heard a tiny voice and
looked down and saw that the Ogre had
changed himself into a brown mouse.
"You see," squeaked the mouse-like Ogre.
"I can change myself into anything. That
is why *everyone* is frightened of me!"
Quick as a flash; before the Ogre could
change back again, Puss killed the mouse.
The Ogre was dead! "Now this castle belongs
to the Marquis of Carabas!" cried Puss.

Puss hurried up the steps into the kitchen.
When the servants of the castle heard that
the Ogre was dead they were so relieved.
"He was such a cruel master," said the butler.
"Well now you have a new master," purred Puss.
"His name is the Marquis of Carabas. You'll
find that the Marquis of Carabas will be a
good and kind master, I promise you!"

"In the next few minutes,"
continued Puss, "the
Royal carriage will
arrive at this castle.
Will you please lay on a feast fit for the
King and his lovely daughter Princess
Rose-Marie, and the Marquis."
When the food was almost ready, Puss
reminded the servants: "Remember, your
new master will arrive soon. And his name
is the Marquis of Carabas!"

When the King arrived with the Princess and Robin, Puss in Boots was there to greet them. "Welcome to the Castle of the Marquis of Carabas!" he purred.

Robin was amazed. Puss seemed to be taking care of everything. And the King and the Princess were happy to accept Robin as the Marquis of Carabas.

Robin and the Princess were so deeply in
love that they had eyes only for each other.
They often went out walking together.
One day Robin asked Princess Rose-Marie to
marry him and she accepted gladly.
Within a year they were married.
And the Marquis of Carabas became Prince
Robin. And Puss, wearing his favourite
boots was the first brides cat; taking the
place of a bridesmaid!

Of course Robin and his Princess lived
happily ever after.
And as for Puss in Boots?
Well...
He was given some Royal boots and a
Royal jacket.
He ate Royal fish, and drank Royal cream.
He slept in a Royal cat basket, and
chased Royal mice.
Some time later, Puss married too.
And the Kingdom was blessed with
Royal kittens!

Snow White
and the Seven Dwarfs

In the heart of a forest stood an old castle...
In the castle lived a King and Queen.
The Queen had a baby daughter called
Snow White. Snow White was a lovely baby
but the Queen was always worried about
Snow White's health.
One day as the Queen was sewing a bonnet for
Snow White, she pricked her finger with the
needle. As the Queen looked at the drop of
blood on her finger she made a wish: "May
our daughter Snow White grow into a

beautiful child. May her hair be as dark as
a raven, and her skin be as white as snow."
Snow White did grow into a lovely child.
But sadly, the Queen died when Snow
White was still a baby.
Later, the King
married again.
This Queen was
beautiful, but vain.
She was also wicked,
and had once been a
witch! She had a
magic mirror which
she often asked:
"Mirror mirror on
the wall,
Who is fairest of us
all?"
The mirror always
answered:
"You are fairest my
Queen!"

One day when the Queen asked her mirror:
"Who is fairest of us all?"
The mirror answered:
"Snow White is fairest of you all!"

At first the Queen couldn't believe what
she had heard.
But the mirror repeated:
"Snow White is fairest of you all!"
The wicked Queen was so angry!

In a rage, she ordered a woodcutter to take
Snow White into the forest and kill her!
Fortunately the woodcutter was a kindly
man. He had no wish to harm a hair on
Snow White's lovely head.
So he told Snow White to run away and hide
from the wicked Queen, and never to go near
the palace again.
After saying 'Goodbye' to the woodcutter,
Snow White walked through the forest.
She walked and walked until she was a long
way from the castle.
On her journey she made friends with the animals.
The birds brought her berries and nuts to eat.
But as the day wore on, Snow White
grew worried. She didn't know where
she was going to shelter for the night...
As it grew dark, Snow White felt very tired.
She was just about to lie down beneath a tree,
when she came to a tiny cottage, almost hidden
under an apple tree...

Snow White walked wearily up the short path
to the front door of the tiny cottage.
She knocked quietly on the door.
In her hand she carried a gift of flowers.
When no one answered, Snow White opened
the door and stepped inside.
She entered a small room...
Around the table were seven little chairs.
Upon the table were seven little cups.
"Who can live here?" gasped Snow White.

Snow White wanted to sit down.
But most of the chairs seemed too small.
She didn't know what to do.
So she went into another room and found
a small bed.
"I do hope no one will mind if I lie
down here," she said.
As she lay on the bed, some of her animal
friends came to keep her company...
Within a minute, Snow White was fast asleep.

She didn't know that the little cottage belonged to seven dwarfs. The dwarfs mined gold in the secret mountain. They worked every day, except Sunday. And even as Snow White slept, they were marching home for tea. The dwarfs were friendly with the animals too. But when a rabbit came to tell them that they had a visitor called Princess Snow White, the dwarfs didn't believe him.

The dwarfs arrived back at their cottage
in the forest and got a surprise!
The rabbit had told the truth!
They *did* have a visitor, and her skin
was as white as snow.
The dwarfs had
just gathered
around Snow
White when
she began
to wake.

The dwarfs just stood and stared at the
beautiful Princess. For a time no one spoke.
"I must be dreaming!" cried Snow White
as she suddenly opened her eyes and saw
the dwarfs standing there.
"Fear not," whispered the eldest dwarf.
"We will not harm you. Tell us what has
brought you to our home in the forest,
and we will try to help you."

"I am a Princess," explained Snow White.
"But my stepmother the Queen wants to kill
me! I walked through the forest all day
looking for somewhere to rest and finally
found your cottage. Please will you help me?"
"Then you must be Princess Snow White!" said
one of the dwarfs. "A rabbit told us about
you. Don't worry. We will shelter you from
the wicked Queen, and take care of you."

The next day, which was Sunday, Snow White
cooked a lovely meal for the seven dwarfs.
Then they all sat by the fire-side and
the dwarfs told tales of the secret
mountain and of trees that could talk.
Snow White did the housework while
they built a chair and bed especially
for her. Sometimes they brought her little
gifts carved of wood and stone.
After a time, Snow White forgot her fear
They were very kind to Snow
White and made a chair and a

bed especially for her, while she
did the housework. Often they
bought her gifts carved
from wood.

Soon, Snow White forgot her fear
of the wicked Queen...

A month passed... Then one day when Snow
White was alone in the cottage, who should
come stealing through the woods – but the
wicked Queen! Once again she had asked
the magic mirror who was the fairest.
When it had replied, "Snow White is fairest!"
the jealous Queen knew that Snow White was
still alive. As the Queen passed through
the forest, even the trees looked unhappy.
Animals fled in fear. Some of the animals

were going to try to warn Snow White, but
the power of the wicked Queen stopped them.
When the wicked Queen came to Snow White's
window, she was disguised as an old woman.
She carried a basket full of ribbons.
"Here's a pretty red ribbon for your dress!"
she cried to Snow White. "Come out and let
me tie it for you."
"You're very kind," smiled Snow White.
"But I'm afraid I can't
afford to buy a

ribbon." "You may *have* the ribbon,"
insisted the wicked Queen. "I have plenty."
"Thank you," smiled Snow White. "The red
ribbon is so pretty."
"Here, let me tie the ribbon for you,"
repeated the disguised Queen.
So Snow White let the Queen tie the ribbon
to her bodice.
But the Queen tied the ribbon so horribly
tight that Snow White could hardly breathe.
Snow White fell to the ground dying.
Luckily, the seven dwarfs came home early
and saved her life by cutting the ribbon.

The wicked Queen
came back the next day.
This time she was
disguised as a gypsy woman.
She tapped on Snow White's window: "I have
a pretty comb for you," she crooned.
Snow White opened the window: "I'd better
not come outside," she said. "The dwarfs
told me to stay indoors."
"Don't worry," muttered the Queen. "I can
place the comb in your hair from here."
So saying, the Queen placed the comb in
Snow White's hair. The comb was poisoned.
As soon as it touched Snow White's head,
she fell to the ground.

When the dwarfs returned they found
Snow White dying. But when the eldest
dwarf saw the strange comb in her hair
he grew suspicious.
As soon as he removed the comb, Snow White
quickly recovered.
"The comb was poisoned," he explained.

"You've saved my life again," smiled
Snow White. "How can I thank you?" "Why
not cook us all our favourite meals
tomorrow night?" suggested one of the dwarfs.

The next day, before the dwarfs set off
for work the eldest dwarf gave a warning
to Snow White.

"The wicked Queen is sure to know that
you are still alive. So you must be *very*
careful. If any strangers come to the
cottage you must not speak to them. Keep all
the windows and doors locked. And let no one
in." Snow White promised to be careful.

114

The dwarfs set out for work in a happy mood,
thinking that Snow White would be safe.
But the wicked Queen came back,
this time disguised as an apple seller.
One of the apples looked so red and juicy,
but in fact one half of the apple was
poisoned. The jealous Queen offered the
apple to Snow White. "Thank you," smiled
Snow White, "but I'd rather not eat it."
"Why ever not my dear?" cried the sly Queen.
"There's nothing wrong with it. I'll take a
bite myself to prove it to you." The Queen
took a bite from the good half of the apple.
Then she handed the apple to Snow White:
"Take a bite from the other side my dear,"
said the wicked Queen. "You'll find it's
the nicest apple you've ever tasted."
Snow White took the apple. "Thank you,"
she smiled. "I love apples, and I'm sure
this apple will be delicious." "Of course
it will my dear," muttered the evil Queen.

Snow White took one bite from the poisoned
half of the apple and fell to the floor
as if dead.
Her animal friends sent a fast flying bird
to fetch the dwarfs.
The dwarfs hurried home as fast as they could.

When the seven dwarfs arrived, they used all
the herbs and medicines they knew to try and
cure Snow White. But Snow White did not
recover. She just lay, silent on the the ground.

"She's dead," said the eldest dwarf at last.
A great sadness hung over the little cottage.

The seven dwarfs made plans for Snow White's
funeral. They were all very upset, but
there was work to be done.
They decided that Snow White should be
buried in a hill top garden, which lay
amongst the secret mountains.
The dwarfs made a glass coffin for
Snow White and laid her inside.
The animals decided to take scented
flowers to brighten her grave.
On the day of the funeral, the dwarfs set
out carrying the glass coffin. It was a
long journey. Nevertheless, many of the
animals went along to pay their last
respects to their friend Snow White.

On the way to the secret mountain, a
handsome Prince rode past. When the prince
saw the beautiful Snow White lying in the
glass coffin, he asked the dwarfs to stop.
One of the dwarfs slipped, and the coffin
banged hard on the ground.
The dwarfs were upset; but only for a while.
The sudden jolt made the piece of poisoned
apple fall out of Snow White's throat!

118

Snow White awoke, as if
from a deep sleep.
The handsome Prince kissed
Princess Snow White's hand.
The dwarfs and the animals
were so delighted!
What started as a funeral
procession was soon to be
a wedding between the
Prince and their
beloved Snow White.

For the wedding,
the seven dwarfs brought
special gifts of gold
and silver from their mine
in the secret mountains.
The animals came to the wedding
bringing fruit and flowers.
And Snow White and the Prince had
a truly happy life together.

As for the wicked Queen...
Well, she grew tired of looking in the
magic mirror: All her wicked deeds had
made her very ugly indeed!

Aladdin and his Wonderful Lamp

A long time ago in China there lived
a little boy called Aladdin.
His father had died when Aladdin was just
a baby. So his mother had to bring him
up alone.
Aladdin lived with his mother in a tiny
hut on the outskirts of the city.
In the distance they could see the many
roofs of the Emperor's palace...

Aladdin's mother was one of the Emperor's washer women. Aladdin did his best to help his mother...

He would collect bundles of dirty laundry from the palace for her to wash.

When the laundry was clean and dry he'd take it back to the palace.

Sometimes he would get a glimpse of the Emperor's daughter whom he liked very much.

He sometimes saw the Emperor's daughter walking in the palace gardens. But it is unlikely that she ever saw Aladdin...

Although Aladdin and his mother worked hard, they were still very poor.

The roof of their hut leaked when it rained. And at times they barely had enough rice to eat. Aladdin often dreamed of having a nice house, and he promised his mother that one day they would have a fine home. But his mother just smiled. Aladdin also dreamed of marrying the Emperor's daughter!

One day, when Aladdin was out walking,
he met a strange looking man.
"I am a magician!" said the man. "And you
are called Aladdin." "That's right!" said
Aladdin. "But how did you know my name?"
"Magic!" cried the Magician. "And with my
magic I can give you and your mother all
the riches you ever dreamed of..."

This was what Aladdin had been longing to
hear: "I would like my mother to live in
a fine house," said Aladdin. "Good!" said the
magician. "But to earn your riches you must
come with me into a secret cave in the
mountains. And in the cave is a precious lamp.
I want *you* to go into the secret cave and fetch
me that precious lamp!"

Only the pure in heart could enter the secret cave. That is why the magician had sent Aladdin! In the cave Aladdin saw many treasures. Just for fun he tried on a golden ring, but when the magician saw this he hissed: "Quick! give me that precious lamp, or I'll leave you in the cave to die!"
"No. Please help me out first," begged Aladdin.
"Then I'll give you the lamp."

But the magician was furious. He closed up the
cave; leaving Aladdin inside to die.
"I'm trapped," thought Aladdin. "There's
no way out. I'll never see my poor mother
again." Aladdin sat down on the stone floor
and began to cry. He twisted his hands
together and as he did so he rubbed the ring
on his finger. The ring was a magic ring.

There was a puff of smoke.
A figure appeared before Aladdin.
"I am the Spirit of the Ring!" said the
figure. "What is your wish?"
"Please take me home!" begged Aladdin.
"And let me take the precious lamp with me."

In an instant, Aladdin found himself back
home. He put the precious lamp in his
mother's room. Then he went out into the
garden to await her return. He still had
the magic ring on his finger. So he wished
for a glimpse of the Emperor's daughter.
The spirit of the Ring granted his wish...

Just for a moment he saw the Emperor's
daughter, walking in the palace gardens.
And it seemed to Aladdin that she was more
beautiful than ever.

Later, when Aladdin showed his mother the
lamp, she said: "It doesn't look like a
precious lamp to me! And what is more
it needs a jolly good clean!" So she went
to the drawer and took out a duster.

As Aladdin's mother polished the lamp,
there was a huge flash of light! followed
by a huge bang, like a clap of thunder.
A great big golden figure appeared before
them saying: "I am the Genie of the Lamp:
What is your command?!"
Aladdin's mother gasped "Now I know why the
magician wanted the lamp. It's a magic lamp!"

The Genie of the Lamp waited until Aladdin
and his mother could think of something
to wish for.
Finally, Aladdin and his mother asked for
great riches. And a grand house with
servants and nice food to eat. "And make
sure the roof doesn't leak!" added Aladdin.
"Your wish is granted!" cried the Genie.
In a moment, Aladdin found himself dressed
in silk and his mother in the finest satin.
After a short while Aladdin invited the
Emperor's daughter to tea.

They fell in love and one day Aladdin went
to the palace and asked the Emperor if he
could marry the Princess. He took the
Emperor a tribute of gold and silver. The
Emperor, who also liked Aladdin, gave his
consent to the marriage.
Aladdin and his Princess settled down and were
living happily together in Aladdin's palace.

Then one day the magician returned.
He was dressed as a pedlar, shouting: "New
lamps for old!"
It was a trick to get the precious lamp!
Aladdin was out. But a servant girl heard
the call. She brought
down the magic lamp
and swopped it for
a shiny tin lamp.

As soon as the magician saw the lamp, he knew it was the magic lamp from the treasure cave. "At last I've found it!" he hissed. "How Aladdin escaped from the cave, I'll never know! But now I'll turn him into a laundry boy again!" After saying this the magician rubbed the lamp.

When the Genie of the Lamp appeared, the magician said: "Take the Princess, and Aladdin's palace, and me to darkest Africa!" "Your wish is my command!" said the Genie. In a very few moments, Aladdin's palace, with the Princess and the magician inside, had landed in darkest Africa!

"This will teach Aladdin to meddle with magic!" laughed the magician. "When he sees that his palace has vanished, he'll wonder if he's been dreaming!"

When Aladdin came home he found that his
palace had disappeared into thin air!
His Princess was nowhere to be seen.
Aladdin sat down and began to cry.
He could not understand what had happened.
Perhaps it had all been a dream?
But after a time, Aladdin remembered the
magic ring that was still on his finger.
So he rubbed it, and the Spirit of the
Ring appeared.

"What is your wish?"
asked the Ring Spirit.

"Please take me to my
Princess!" pleaded Aladdin.
And off they went.

The Princess was
overjoyed to see Aladdin.
"I never thought I'd see
you again!" she cried.
Aladdin asked what
happened. She explained:
"The magician has got the
magic lamp. He made a wish, and we flew here
from China. It was most amazing!"

Aladdin hid until the magician was asleep.
Then he crept up and took back the lamp.
Aladdin rubbed the precious lamp and the
Genie asked once again: "What is your
command?" " Take the Princess, the palace,
and me *back* to China," said Aladdin.
"What about the magician?" asked the Genie.
"Please leave him here!" said the Princess.

The Genie of the Lamp granted their wish.

Aladdin and his Princess found themselves back in their palace in China. The first thing Aladdin did was to take the precious lamp and hide it.

When the magician woke
up, he was all alone in Africa.
"Oh dear!" he sighed. " That's
the trouble with magic... you
never know what will happen next!"

ISBN 0 86163 130 7

© Award Publications Limited 1985
Spring House, Spring Place   London NW5 3BH

Printed in Belgium